Santa's Christmas UNICORN

MORTIMER

Published in 2020 by Mortimer Children's Books
An Imprint of Welbeck Children's Limited,
part of Welbeck Publishing Group.
20 Mortimer Street London W1T 3JW

Text & Illustrations © Welbeck Children's Limited,
part of Welbeck Publishing Group.

Author: Alex Allan
Illustrator: Samantha Meredith
Art editor: Deborah Vickers
Editor: Jenni Lazell

ISBN 978-1-83935-031-3

Printed in Heshan, China
10 9 8 7 6 5 4 3 2 1

It was the night before Christmas
and all through the land . . .

All the tables were laid,
and the fun had been planned.

The children rested sleepy heads
All tucked up in their cozy beds,
Dreaming of the gifts to come,
Their empty stockings carefully hung.

Meanwhile . . . over in the far North Pole,
Things weren't quite so under control.
The workshop elves had toiled for weeks,
They'd stacked and sorted in their sleep.

SANTA'S
WORKSHOP

But still the backlog grew and grew—
The list was endless. What could they do?

The ribbons were all tangled,
the paper was fighting back!

I QUIT!

The elves were reaching
breaking point.
Their nerves were
about to crack!

Santa was in the stables,
Trying to calm the reindeer down,
Dasher was looking furious,
while Prancer wore a frown.

Rudolph put his hoof down
and refused to pull the sleigh,
He yelled "We won't work overtime,
and give us extra hay!"

Santa had a headache,
his nerves were feeling frayed.
Things had never been so hectic,
never so delayed.

He went to check the engine
on his dear old trusty sleigh.
But even that was broken!
It wasn't Santa's day.

You've got
to be kidding!

By now his head was throbbing,
his mind was in a haze.
He had a look at what the kids
were asking for these days . . .

"I WANT A CHRISTMAS

⭐ **Bobby, 4 years old (good)**
- Flying drone
- Cell phone (a new one just like Dad's)
- Other toys (you can choose) ✓

⭐ **Milly, 6 years old (also good)**
- Rollerblades
- Trampoline
- Sparkly crown and matching dress ✓
- A real-life Christmas unicorn (that flies)

⭐ **Billy, 6 years old (good)**
- Games console
- Racing bike (red) ✓
- Remote controlled boat
- Toys and games

The elves went sadly to their jobs,
they sewed and hammered through their sobs.

So many toys to make today . . .
Oh, who could help them save the day?

Then softly through the chaos,
they heard a distant sound,
And a misty swirl of sparkles
fell gently all around.

Look there! Appearing in a glow of light,
His coat a-shimmer, his eyes so bright . . .

He tossed his mane and stamped a foot—
The presents were neatly wrapped.

And suddenly, as if by magic,
The sleigh was tightly packed!

Santa's smile grew broader,
he grinned from ear to ear.
"Move over Rudolph Reindeer,
you're the co-pilot this year!"

He climbed up front and
grabbed the reins, he was all set to go!
A unicorn for Christmas,
A ho ho ho ho

HOOOOOO

And if you'd been a-peeking
(which you never, NEVER should)
You'd have seen a special sight that night,
As Santa took his Christmas flight.

For galloping across the sky,
Hooves like lightning, head held high,
Was Santa's Christmas unicorn,
pulling the shining sleigh,
Glittering, shimmering, glistening,
as he led them on their way.

Ho ho ho and a
very merry Chistmas!